Hello, Family Members,

Learning to read is one of the most important accomplishments of early childhood. **Hello Reader!** books are designed to help children become skilled readers who like to read. Beginning readers learn to read by remembering frequently used words like "the," "is," and "and"; by using phonics skills to decode new words; and by interpreting picture and text clues. These books provide both the stories children enjoy and the structure they need to read fluently and independently. Here are suggestions for helping your child *before*, *during*, and *after* reading:

Before

- Look at the cover and pictures and have your child predict what the story is about.
- Read the story to your child.
- Encourage your child to chime in with familiar words and phrases.
- Echo read with your child by reading a line first and having your child read it after you do.

During

- Have your child think about a word he or she does not recognize right away. Provide hints such as "Let's see if we know the sounds" and "Have we read other words like this one?"
- Encourage your child to use phonics skills to sound out new words.
- Provide the word for your child when more assistance is needed so that he or she does not struggle and the experience of reading with you is a positive one.
- Encourage your child to have fun by reading with a lot of expression . . . like an actor!

After

- Have your child keep lists of interesting and favorite words.
- Encourage your child to read the books over and over again. Have him or her read to brothers, sisters, grandparents, and even teddy bears. Repeated readings develop confidence in young readers.
- Talk about the stories. Ask and answer questions. Share ideas about the funniest and most interesting characters and events in the stories.

I do hope that you and your child enjoy this book.

—Francie Alexander
Reading Specialist,
Scholastic's Learning Ventures

To Natalie, Nicole, Christopher, and Austin
— KP

To Nikolai
— JJM

Published by Scholastic Inc. SCHOLASTIC, HELLO READER,
CARTWHEEL BOOKS and associated logos are trademarks and/or
registered trademarks of Scholastic Inc.

Library of Congress Cataloging-in-Publication Data
Puckett, Kelley.
    Batman's dark secret / by Kelley Puckett ; illustrated by Jon J Muth.
       p.   cm.— (Hello reader! Level 3)
    Summary: The orphan boy Bruce Wayne conquers his fear of the dark, making it possible for him to grow up and become the crime-fighting hero Batman.
    ISBN 0-439-09551-4
    [1. Fear of the dark Fiction. 2. Orphans Fiction. 3. Heroes Fiction]
  I. Muth, Jon J, ill. II. Title. III. Series.
PZ7.P94967Pat   2000
[E]—dc21   99-15262
                                     CIP

12 11 10 9 8 7 6 5 4 3 2   9/9 0/0 01 02 03 04

Printed in the U.S.A.   23
First printing, October 1999

BATMAN'S DARK SECRET

by Kelley Puckett

Illustrated by Jon J Muth

Hello Reader! — Level 3

SCHOLASTIC INC.   Cartwheel ·B·O·O·K·S·®

New York   Toronto   London   Auckland   Sydney
Mexico City   New Delhi   Hong Kong

Nothing scares Batman. Nothing at all, not even the dark. But it's not because he's big and strong.

It's because he knows a secret. A secret he learned long ago, when he was just a little boy named Bruce Wayne. . . .

It was a cold night in Gotham City,
but Bruce didn't care. It was movie night,
his favorite night of all.

The hero had a cape and a mask and a sword. He fought evil, and he won.

Bruce wanted to be just like him.

Walking home, they came
to an alley. It was pitch black,
darker than dark.

But Bruce was young and brave,
and his parents were with him.
He wasn't afraid of the dark.

First he heard loud voices, then a bang. There was a flash of light, and the smell of smoke.

Then again—
the bang, the flash,
the smoke.

And when he came out of the dark,
he was alone. His parents were gone!

Bruce lived far outside the city
in a very big house. It looked even
bigger now.

Alfred was the butler. He took care
of Bruce. When Bruce complained
the house was dark, Alfred knew
what to do.

He put lights in the library. He put lights in the halls.

He put lights, lamps, and candles all over the walls.

Bruce wouldn't sleep until the whole house was bright. "No darkness," he told Alfred. "No darkness," he whispered in his dreams.

Bruce began to take long walks
through the countryside. He'd sit by
his favorite tree for hours, thinking
about nothing at all.

One day the sun was extra bright, and Bruce was extra tired. Before he knew it, he'd fallen asleep. And by the time he woke up, it was getting dark.

Bruce ran and ran. The sun sank lower. The sky grew darker. Bruce ran faster.

He didn't see the hole. His foot
went in, then his leg, then him.

He was falling in darkness. Down,
down into the dark, a dark that made
the moonlight bright.

WHAM! He landed hard on cold, wet stone. His ankle hurt, and he was scared.

Then the darkness came alive.
It screeched, it clawed, it swarmed
around him. He ran and tripped
and fell to the ground.

Slowly, slowly, his eyes adjusted. The darkness became . . . bats. Tiny, little bats. Bruce wasn't afraid of bats.

Then he saw it.

Not a bat. Too big. It was a monster, and it was coming for him.

Its hot breath fell on his face.
The wind from its wings blew back
his hair. His fist found a stick and
before he could think . . .

"NO!"

The monster . . .
backed away.

It was scared . . .
of him.

Bruce felt strange, somehow. Different.

He would grow up.
He would fight evil and win.

And he would never be afraid again.